A Note to Parents and Caregivers:

Read-it! Readers are for children who are just starting on the amazing road to reading. These beautiful books support both the acquisition of reading skills and the love of books.

 The PURPLE LEVEL presents basic topics and objects using high frequency words and simple language patterns.

 The RED LEVEL presents familiar topics using common words and repeating sentence patterns.

 The BLUE LEVEL presents new ideas using a larger vocabulary and varied sentence structure.

 The YELLOW LEVEL presents more challenging ideas, a broad vocabulary, and wide variety in sentence structure.

 The GREEN LEVEL presents more complex ideas, an extended vocabulary range, and expanded language structures.

 The ORANGE LEVEL presents a wide range of ideas and concepts using challenging vocabulary and complex language structures.

When sharing a book with your child, read in short stretches, pausing often to talk about the pictures. Have your child turn the pages and point to the pictures and familiar words. And be sure to reread favorite stories or parts of stories.

There is no right or wrong way to share books with children. Find time to read with your child, and pass on the legacy of literacy.

Adria F. Klein, Ph.D.
Professor Emeritus
California State University
San Bernardino, California

Editor: Jacqueline A. Wolfe
Page Production: Amy Bailey Muehlenhardt
Creative Director: Keith Griffin
Editorial Director: Carol Jones
Managing Editor: Catherine Neitge
The illustrations in this book were created with watercolor and colored pencil.

Picture Window Books
5115 Excelsior Boulevard
Suite 232
Minneapolis, MN 55416
877-845-8392
www.picturewindowbooks.com

Printed in the United States of America.

Library of Congress Cataloging-in-Publication Data
Klein, Adria F.
Max goes shopping / by Adria F. Klein ; illustrated by Mernie Gallagher-Cole.
p. cm. — (Read-it! readers)
Summary: Max enjoys shopping at a variety of stores.
ISBN 1-4048-1177-X (hardcover)
[1. Shopping— Fiction.] I. Gallagher-Cole, Mernie, ill. II. Title. III. Series.

PZ7.K678324Mak 2005
[E]—dc22   2005003784

Max
Goes Shopping

by Adria F. Klein
illustrated by Mernie Gallagher-Cole

Special thanks to our advisers for their expertise:

Adria F. Klein, Ph.D.
Professor Emeritus, California State University
San Bernardino, California

Susan Kesselring, M.A.
Literacy Educator
Rosemount-Apple Valley-Eagan (Minnesota) School District

PICTURE WINDOW BOOKS
Minneapolis, Minnesota

Max likes to go shopping.

Max goes to the shoe store.

He gets some blue shoes.

Max goes to the clothing store.

He gets a red shirt.

Max goes to the bookstore.

He gets a book about trucks.

Max goes to the sports store.

He gets a baseball and a glove.

Max goes to the school supply
store. He gets a new notebook and
some pencils.

15

Max goes to the ice cream store.

He gets a chocolate cone.

Max goes to the video store.

NEW RELEASES

He gets a video about dogs.

Max goes home.

He is tired from shopping.

Max likes to go shopping.

More *Read-it!* Readers

Bright pictures and fun stories help you practice your reading skills. Look for more books at your level.

A Year of Fun by Susan Blackaby
Ann Plants a Garden by Susan Blackaby
Bess and Tess by Susan Blackaby
Dan Gets Set by Susan Blackaby
Max Goes on the Bus by Adria F. Klein
Max Goes to School by Adria F. Klein
Max Goes to the Barber by Adria F. Klein
Max Goes to the Dentist by Adria F. Klein
Max Goes to the Library by Adria F. Klein
The Best Soccer Player by Susan Blackaby
Wes Gets a Pet by Susan Blackaby
Winter Fun for Kat by Susan Blackaby

Looking for a specific title or level? A complete list of *Read-it!* Readers is available on our Web site:
www.picturewindowbooks.com